Lilac peabody

and
Honeysuckle Hope

ANNIE DALTON

Illustrated by Griff

HarperCollins *Children's Books*

First published in Great Britain by HarperCollins *Children's Books* in 2005
HarperCollins *Children's Books* is a division of HarperCollins*Publishers* Ltd
77-85 Fulham Palace Road, Hammersmith, London W6 8JB

The HarperCollins *Children's Books* website address is
www.harpercollinschildrensbooks.co.uk

I

Text copyright © Annie Dalton 2005
Illustrations © Andrew Griffin 2005

ISBN 0 00 713774 5

The author and illustrator assert the moral right
to be identified as author and illustrator of the work.

Printed and bound in England by
Clays Ltd, St Ives plc

3 8043 26829305 3

Also by Annie Dalton:

Lilac Peabody and Sam Sparks
Lilac Peabody and Bella Bright
Lilac Peabody and Charlie Chase

The *Mel Beeby: Agent Angels* series:

Keeping It Real
Winging It
Losing the Plot
Flying High
Calling the Shots
Fogging Over
Fighting Fit
Making Waves
Budding Star

1.
Honey Against The World!

This story starts with a blob.

A bald stinky little blob in a hospital cot, a few weeks before Christmas.

"How do you like your brother, Honey?" smiles

my stepmum Ellie.

"He smells like mice," I say in my coldest voice.

Ellie picks up the little Blob and sniffs his rear end. "I don't believe it!" she groans. "This little rascal needs changing again."

"Let me!" says Dad, as if people are queuing up. He starts unpopping poppers on the Blob's tiny sleep suit. "We're calling him Joe," he beams.

"Don't you think Joe Hope is a great name?"

"It's your kid," I mutter. "Call it what you like."

"Apart from the mouse smell," Ellie says brightly. "What do you think of the new member of the family?"

I tell my dad, "I'll be in the waiting room."

The waiting room is down the corridor. I ignore the dads and grannies reading magazines and go to look at the fish tank.

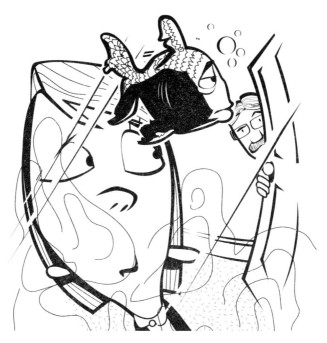

I'm interested in fish. I've got a fish tank in my bedroom, but I take care of mine. This one hasn't been cleaned for weeks. The water is turning into green gravy. The fish look so unhappy that I'm scared I'm going to cry.

Dad comes up behind me. "Are you OK?"

I quickly wipe my eyes. "No I'm not!" I growl. "This tank is disgusting!"

Dad puts his arm round me. "This is a big change for you. Ellie and I realise that."

"These people don't care about fish!" I rant. "They want a pretty background for visitors. Well, fish aren't a background! They're real!"

My dad isn't even listening. "But some changes are for the better," he says. "Marrying Ellie, having Joe, these are good changes. It's a new start, Honey."

"Dad, these *fish* are sick! You've got to tell someone."

My dad sounds stressed. "OK. I'll ask the nurse to clean the tank. Listen, Honey, I just want you to know you'll always be my special little Honey Bun, even if Ellie and I have five children."

"They're going to DIE, Dad!" I scream. "Don't you even CARE!"

When I get home I fly upstairs to check on my fish.

They're fine, swimming around happy as anything.

My fish are beautiful, like teeny-tiny rainbows, and they're smart too. They read each other's minds! They swim SO fast, yet they always manage to change direction at the exact same moment.

When I die I'm coming back as a fish. We'll go everywhere in a happy rainbow-coloured gang, and the other fish will never think bad things about me.

I press my face against the cool glass of the aquarium.

Two little fish swim up and give me fishy kisses

through the glass. They wouldn't do that would they, if I was a bad person? I think they understand I'm just doing my best.

That's what Miss May told the class, when we started in the juniors. "The wonderful thing about Honey is she always does her best."

She doesn't think I'm so wonderful any more.

At the last parent-teacher evening, she said, "Mr Hope, I'm concerned about Honey's behaviour. She is extremely aggressive. None of

the other children will play with her."

Dad said, "I thought she was friends with Lara and Bella?"

"She was," sighed Miss May. "Who knows what happened there? That little girl is just at war with the whole world."

Neither of them noticed the door wasn't closed. They didn't know I'd heard every word.

It's not true what Miss May said.

I'm not at war with the whole world. It's only humans I can't stand.

When we collect Ellie and the Blob from the hospital, the Blob screams all the way home in the car.

The instant Dad unlocks our front door I push past and run up to my room.

All day, Ellie and Dad try to get me to come out.

"Won't you help me bath him?" wheedles Ellie. "I'm new to this. I could use some help."

She and Dad use a special voice when they talk to me these days, like I'll explode if they speak to me like a normal person.

At bedtime Dad comes in to ask if I'd like him to read me a story.

I roll my eyes. "Newsflash, Dad! I've been able to read since I was six."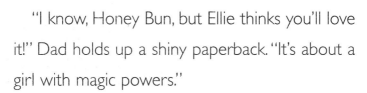

"I know, Honey Bun, but Ellie thinks you'll love it!" Dad holds up a shiny paperback. "It's about a girl with magic powers."

"I *hate* those stories," I snap. "Everybody knows kids have NO power whatsoever. We have to do everything you tell us! But instead of telling the truth, writers make up stories about kids with amazing superpowers."

Dad looks startled. "Oh, right. Well, erm, I'll just leave it there in case you change your mind."

Ellie comes in. The Blob is draped limply over her shoulder, making piggy grunts. "You two having fun?" she beams.

"Your baby's leaking," I say coldly.

Ellie squints down at the baby sick trickling down her sleeve. "Oh, no! I just put this on!" She starts dabbing with a tissue.

"Honey was telling me she doesn't believe in magic," Dad says. He sounds slightly hurt.

"Really?" says my stepmum in surprise. "Haven't you ever made a birthday wish when you blew out your candles?"

"Don't remember," I growl.

"I'm a sucker for magic," Ellie smiles. "I'm a big kid at heart."

"That's why I love you!" says Dad mushily.

He kisses her nose then Ellie kisses his nose.

"This IS still my room," I protest.

But they're in a little world of their own and they don't hear. Now they're kissing little Blobby.

It's like they've forgotten I exist.

2.
Seven Perfect Birthdays

I was fibbing to Ellie.

I used to believe in magic. And I used to love my birthdays.

I remember every birthday wish I've ever

made and I remember every birthday present and every single birthday cake.

Obviously I loved getting presents, but the best part of my birthday was always when Mum brought in my cake with its flickering candles – my real mum I'm talking about now.

Mum would say, "You mustn't tell your wish or it won't come true!" And Dad would say, "Quickly! Before the candles burn out!" And I'd scrunch up my face and blow out all my candles in one go…

I had seven perfect birthdays.

My eighth birthday looked set to be the best ever.

That was the year I got the aquarium. It was going to be a surprise, but Mum thought it would be fun if we went to buy it together; that way I could pick out the most interesting rocks and water plants. Mum even let me get a shipwreck with pirate treasure!

That year Mum baked my cake well before the big day. I pestered her to let me see it but she wouldn't even let me peek, so I knew it had to be special.

A few days before my birthday, my mum was in a car crash and got rushed to hospital in an ambulance. It was the worst thing that had ever happened. I kept asking when she was coming home but Dad said it might take a long time for her to recover.

On my birthday I made Dad take my mystery cake into the hospital. I said Mum would be upset if we celebrated my birthday without her. Dad agreed. Probably we had the same idea. If we did everything like normal then my mum would get better.

But when we reached the hospital my mum didn't look better. She just lay there. She didn't even smile.

As Dad lifted my cake out of its tin, the nurses clapped.

I just gasped. My mum had baked me an aquarium cake! She'd decorated it with marzipan fish and sweetie shells and pebbles to make it look exactly like my aquarium. There was even a shipwreck with treasure. There was just one difference. Mum had added a plastic mermaid. That was our joke. Mum used to call me her little mermaid because of my long hair.

I remember thinking I'd have to wash off the icing before I put the mermaid in my aquarium. And I remember I got annoyed with my dad because he took too long to light the candles. His hands were trembling so the match kept burning out.

When the candles were lit I smiled at my mum, wanting her to say, "You must never tell your wish," like she did every birthday.

She didn't say a word.

"Your mum's feeling tired," a nurse said softly.

"Quickly! Before your candles go out!" Dad told me, but his voice was trembling the same as his hands.

I puffed up my cheeks and blew out my candles.

I never told one single person what I wished. But it didn't make any difference. My mum died the next day.

Dad and I didn't know what to do next.

After the funeral we just camped in the sitting room, watching DVDs.

I stopped bothering to brush my hair and Dad started forgetting to tell me when it was time for bed. He'd wait till I fell asleep then carry me upstairs like a baby. This went on for weeks.

One night Dad carried me upstairs as usual and, as usual, I woke up the instant he put me in my bed.

I waited till he went downstairs again, then I tiptoed over to my aquarium and lifted out the little dripping mermaid. I don't know why I did that. Maybe I was going to kiss her?

I flung her on the ground and stamped on her. Strange sounds came out of my mouth. It wasn't like normal crying. I don't know what it was, but I was scaring myself so I made myself stop.

I whimpered, "I wish… I wish—"

"Shut up," I told myself. "It's too late for wishes. There's no such thing as magic."

Someone must have been listening. There was a fizzing sound like when somebody lights a sparkler and a silvery shimmer filled my room.

"It's never too late for magic, Honey!" said a strange little voice.

I went rigid with shock.

"*What's that?*" I said in a hoarse whisper, then I scooted frantically to the end of my bed and pulled up the covers so just my eyes peeked over.

"Go away!" I told it shakily.

But my room just got brighter and even more shimmery.

The fish peered out from their tank with amazed expressions.

You'd probably have been amazed too.

I just felt all mixed up. Actually I felt like I wanted to cry.

"Yes, it IS too late for magic," I hissed. "I wished and I wished but now my mum is dead."

"That's why I came to help you—" began the voice.

"You can't help me! No one can. So just go away!"

"Wouldn't you like to meet me first?" wheedled the voice.

A shimmery shape started to form at the bottom of my bed.

I backed away. "I don't want to meet you!" I gabbled. "I don't want ANYTHING to do with magic. Magic is rubbish. Push off!"

My visitor seemed puzzled. "So why did you make a wish?"

"I… I made a mistake," I stuttered.

"I don't think you made a mistake," it contradicted. "I think you need a friend."

"I do NOT need a friend, specially not a magic friend," I hissed. "I'm banning you and your stupid magic from this room, so beat it!"

The voice sounded disappointed. "I respect your wishes of course. But I won't give up. Real friends hang on in no matter what."

"Can't hear you!" I sang. "La la la!"

The shimmery shape began to fade.

"Good!" I said fiercely. "And don't you *dare* come back!"

3.
A Fresh Start

Next day I was woken by the sound of my dad vacuuming.

Downstairs, cold air blasted through the house. Dad had opened all the windows. I ran into the kitchen. The takeaway cartons had gone. There was a row of plastic bags out by the bin. Dad was just tying up the last sack.

I shivered in the draught. "What's going on, Dad?"

"It's time to get on with our lives," he told me. "It's what your mum would want. There'll be no more sleeping on the sofa and we'll only eat takeaway on Saturday nights. Now get dressed, Honey Bun, and comb your hair."

"I can't," I whimpered. "It's too messy now."

Dad couldn't comb my hair either.

"No problem," he said. "We'll just cut the tangles out."

I almost cried when I saw my weird new hairstyle, but my dad was trying his best, so I gulped, "Thanks, Dad."

Next Dad said we had to go into town to buy some real food.

We hadn't been to a supermarket for ages. We got a bit carried away, but when we unpacked the bags at home, my dad looked shocked. "We spent a fortune but we haven't got any actual meals!"

"Next time make a list," I told him. "Mum always made a list. And you have to put, like, green vegetables and fresh orange juice and rice."

I thought if we did everything the same as when Mum was alive, I could just about cope. So that's what we did. I went back to school and Dad went back to his office.

Saturday afternoons we'd go out somewhere like the zoo. I didn't care just so long as it was somewhere we'd been with Mum. Even though we only went to familiar places, I was relieved when Saturday night came. The scary stuff was over and we could have takeaway and watch DVDs.

On Sunday mornings Dad took me for breakfast at Otto's, Mum's favourite cafe. I couldn't usually manage my breakfast but I could drink all my hot chocolate if I did it in tiny sips.

Dad would give me the cartoon section to read while he caught up with the news. I made a point of laughing at the cartoons. I knew my dad wanted me to enjoy myself.

Afterwards we'd go home and Dad would try to cook a Sunday roast, but cooking was more Mum's thing. Dad only cooked five dishes in those days and three of them used melted cheese.

I HATE melted cheese.

That's why Dad started going to cookery classes.

Guess who was teaching Dad's class?

Ellie.

Dad and I were doing OK together. We didn't need anyone else; that's what I thought anyway. But as the weeks went by, Dad talked about Ellie more and more, telling me how well the two of them got on.

They must have done. Six months after they met he married her.

Granny Hope made me a hideous pink

bridesmaid's dress with fiddly hooks down the back that she had to do up for me.

"Try to smile, Honeysuckle," she said, brightly. "You didn't want your dad to be alone his whole life, surely?"

"He wasn't alone. He had me," I whispered.

I had to walk behind Dad and Ellie, smiling a fake smile and holding a bunch of pink rosebuds. Everything was pink at their wedding, except Dad's suit and Ellie's dress, which was the colour of vanilla ice cream. I kept thinking, *soon I'll wake up*. But the bad dream just went on.

At the reception, my face felt stiff from all that smiling, so I crept under a table for a rest. The pink tablecloth turned my hiding place into a rosy cave. It felt peaceful under there. I pretended the wedding guests' voices were far-off waves.

"I wish I could just stay here and never come out," I whispered.

There was a fizzing sound and my cave lit up with silvery light. "That's the most depressing

wish I've ever heard!" said a familiar voice. "And I've heard a LOT of wishes!"

I spun round so fast I banged my head. A weird shimmery little person was trying to form. I could see shimmery fairy-sized shoes and a pair of tiny shimmery wings. I couldn't see a face, but I didn't want to either!

"Are you absolutely sure you don't want me to be your friend?" it asked hopefully.

The little creature's shape was getting clearer. I could make out strange glittery clothes and little plaits with flowers braided into them.

I backed out of my hiding place in a panic.

"I don't want to see you!" I shrieked. "I KEEP telling you, I DON'T need any FRIENDS!"

Everybody stopped talking. Dad, Ellie and loads of strangers were all staring at me.

I shot back under the table. To my relief the fairy had gone.

In its place was a small shimmery card.
It said:

On the back someone had scribbled:

I tore it up and threw it on the floor.

4.

The Baddest Girl In The School.

I wasn't always Honey No-Mates.

When Mum was alive I had loads of friends. But these days everyone at school acts as if I'm some hideous monster. They're like, "Oh, Honey is so mean nowadays! Why can't she be nice again?" As if they're the only ones who have feelings!

No one wants to hear my side. You won't believe this, but after my mum died all my friends blanked me.

It's true. I used to be best friends with Lara, but after I lost my mum, she totally changed. Every time she saw me, she'd scuttle out of my way. It was like I had a deadly disease.

As the weeks went by I got really churned up, until I felt like I was ready to explode. I didn't feel like a person any more. I felt like a volcano full of boiling lava.

One day, without warning, all my upset feelings boiled over at once, and I said the one thing I knew would hurt Lara's feelings.

I said, "I bet you were so cute when you were little, before you put on all that fat and blubber!" Then I ran off laughing.

I didn't know this before, but I've got a real talent for hurting people. I know just how to get under their skins. And when I do it right, when I really make them cry, I feel brilliant; and for a while, my boiling-hot feelings go away and I feel like the old sweet Honey, the Little Mermaid Honey.

Well, you didn't think I turned into a bully *overnight* did you?

I was only a little bit mean to begin with and I usually said sorry.

Then one day a new girl joined our class called Bella. Some kids started picking on her just because she's a circus kid. So I went up to the bullies and sorted them out.

After that Bella and I started going around together. It was nice having someone to do stuff with again.

Then Dad and Ellie announced they were having the Blob.

I couldn't believe it. First he marries a total stranger, then he wants a *baby* with her! My dad had got himself a completely new life without even thinking about me!

I decided I was going to get a new life too. I was going to run away with Bella when the circus left town!

OK, I knew I couldn't just run away – I'd have to find a way to earn some money – but I'd always fancied the idea of being a juggler, so I asked Bella to teach me. I didn't tell her why but she seemed thrilled. "You should come to our circus school," she beamed. "My Auntie Fran is an ace juggling teacher."

My first circus skills lesson went brilliantly. Bella's auntie said I was a natural juggler. I started going back with Bella after school so we could perfect our routine.

Bella's auntie was so impressed with our double act that she asked us to perform at a show the circus students were putting on.

I should have known it was too good to be true. Bella waited until we were out under the lights with everyone watching, then she knocked over the table with all our juggling stuff and ran out! She left me alone in front of all those people! Everyone was staring. It was worse than the wedding. I wanted the earth to open up and swallow me.

Afterwards Bella made up some story about getting stage fright. All I knew was that she'd ruined my one chance of a happy life.

I got her back though. I told everyone I broke friends with Bella because her family were dirty thieves who lived on dog food.

I told you I'm ace at hurting people.

"Honey Hope, the baddest girl in the school." That's what the other kids started calling me. It was like I'd turned into an evil baddie, Honey the Bully, and now I couldn't turn back.

5.
Magic Is Banned For Ever!

This story started with the Blob because since then my life has been a total nightmare. First I lose Mum, then I lose my friends and then on top of all that I have to share my home with a stinky screamy little Blob. And as if that isn't bad enough, we have to have an Ellie-style Christmas.

"Wow," Dad says, when he sees what Ellie has done to our Christmas tree. "I don't think we've had *pink* decorations before, have we, Honey?"

"Only in our nightmares," I say under my breath.

On Christmas morning, Dad and Ellie pretend to be excited as they unwrap another squeaky toy. Like, "Ooh, what's this, Joe! OMIGOSH!! It's a pointless purple plastic thingy!!"

The Blob just says "Goo," and dribbles milk on to its bib.

"DO cheer up, Honey-suckle!" Gran sighs.

Ellie and Gran spend all morning in the kitchen.

My real mum was really relaxed about Christmas dinner. It was ready when it was ready. If I got hungry I just snacked on chocolate money!

But my stepmum has our roast turkey, plus all the trimmings, on the table at one o'clock precisely.

"Doesn't this look fabulous, Honey?" Dad asks me.

"If you like big dead birds," I say.

And I kick over my chair and run out.

Have you ever had those dreams where you dream you're asleep, and then you dream you wake up?

Maybe you only get them when you're upset? Because I have one of those on Christmas night.

In my dream I'm woken by a bright light

shining in through my curtains. I stumble to the window in time to see a little blue-green shooting star whizzing towards our house. To my astonishment it zooms in through my open window. You'd think it would burn the rug, but it just lies sparkling quietly like a handful of diamonds.

I'm wondering if I dare to touch it, when WHOOSH! The star turns into the weird little fairy I almost saw at the wedding.

"Nice to meet you at last!"

she smiles.

"I'm Lilac Peabody!"

"Fibber!" I growl. "No one in this world is called Lilac Peabody."

She laughs. "Who said I was from this world?"

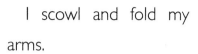

I scowl and fold my arms.

Lilac seems impressed. "Wow, you're even mad in your dreams!"

"I don't have to be nice if I don't want!" I snarl.

She lands on my pillow with a bounce.

"You've got an unusual name yourself, Honeysuckle Hope!"

"This is just a stupid dream, you know! I won't even remember you in the morning."

Lilac Peabody is still bouncing on my pillow, as if it's a bouncy castle.

"You're not even pretty," I say rudely. "Fairies are supposed to be pretty."

Lilac looks surprised. "Did I say I was a fairy?"

"What are you then?" I sneer. "An undersized troll?"

"Nah! A troll would have eaten you by now!" she chuckles. "Just think of me as a friendly magic busybody."

I clench my fists. "I keep on telling you! I don't believe in MAGIC, and I don't NEED friends, especially some ugly little troll-fairy!"

"That's where you're wrong," she sighs. "You're the loneliest child I've ever met. Your best friends are *fishes*, Honey!"

"SO!" I shout. "What's it got to do with YOU, Lily Beanbody, or whatever your stupid name is?"

"Ssh! You'll wake yourself up. Then I really will have to go. I can only visit you in your dream bedroom at the moment because you made your real bedroom into a magic-free zone."

"It still is! Magic is banned from my room for EVER!"

And I wake up.

I'm in my real bedroom in the middle of a real dark night.

And I'm all alone, yelling my heart out.

6.
Little Boy Pink

Lilac stays away after that and life returns to normal. As normal as life can be when a Blob's taken over your family and you've got no friends.

On our first day back at school we have to do acrostics.

An acrostic is a poem where you use the letters of someone's name to start each line. Miss May says we have to write an acrostic about someone we know really well.

I decide to write about the Blob, also known as Joe Hope.

This is my poem.

J oe's nappies have an

O bnoxious odour that is worse than

E ggy burps.

H is face is an ugly red blob.

'O' is the shape his mouth goes when he
     screams.

P oo, pee and puke, that's all he does.

E uw!

Miss May goes all flustered. "I'm glad you know how to use the word 'obnoxious', dear, but did you have to be so unkind?"

I shrug. "You never said it had to be kind, Miss."

"We did acrostics today," I tell Ellie when we get home. "I wrote about Joe. Want to see?"

Her face lights up. "I'd love to!"

Ellie's face changes as she reads my poem. She takes a breath. "I know what you're doing, Honey, but it's not going to work. Joe and I are here to stay. Nothing you can do will change that."

I stomp up to my room. Nothing I can do, huh? That's like declaring war. Well, if Ellie wants a war, she can have one.

I pick up the book Dad and Ellie bought me, the one about the girl with magic powers, and pull a horrible face at the cover. Then, in a flash, I know how to hit back!

I'm going to make my stepmum sorry she was ever born.

I find Ellie downstairs writing her schedule for the next day.

8.15 – Take Honey to school

9.00 – Go to gym

10.30 – Meet Katie for coffee

My stepmum is a complete control-freak! She wants life to be all smooth and samey like those icky low fat yoghurts she likes. What my stepmum hates is nasty surprises.

Bad luck Ellie!

I say sweetly, "Mummy?"

I've never called her "Mummy" before. Ellie looks as if she's going to cry.

I put on a girly little voice. "I've just read that book you got me, Mummy. It's brilliant! That girl is so like me it's unreal!"

"I'm glad!" she says warmly. "How sweet of you to tell me."

"Can I tell you a secret? It's a bit weird."

"You can tell me anything, sweetie, you know that!"

I look down at my shoes. "I think I've got special powers too, like that girl in the book."

"Wow!" my stepmum says. "What kind of powers?"

I give her a spooky smile. "I'm not sure yet. I just thought you should be warned."

I run up to my room and do a little war dance in front of my fish tank. Sometimes being bad is SO much fun!

The next few months I do everything I can to wind Ellie up.

For instance my stepmum has a system for laundry, where we put different types of dirty washing into separate bags.

One morning I sneak one of my red socks into the Blob's white wash. I wish I could see Ellie's face when she realises her precious Little Boy Blue has been changed into Little Boy Pink!

"But we use different *bags*," she wails to Dad at teatime. "I can't think how it happened!"

"I don't see why you're upset," I say in an innocent voice. "Isn't pink your favourite colour?"

My stepmum comes into the bathroom as I'm brushing my teeth. "It was you, wasn't it?" she says quietly. "Don't deny it."

"I didn't *mean* to," I whine. "I tried to tell you I had special powers, but you wouldn't listen."

A few nights later I get up and change all the clocks.

I change Dad and Ellie's watches. I even change the time on their mobiles. Then I creep back to bed.

Next morning, Ellie gazes around the empty school playground in bewilderment. "Where is everyone?"

The church clock starts to strike. I deliberately count each chime aloud. "Gosh, Mummy, I'm an hour late!" I gasp. "I'll get in SO much trouble!" I pull a sad face. "Oh, no, will you be late meeting your friend?"

My stepmum sighs as if she's really tired. "Honey, why do you have to do these things?"

"It's my powers," I whimper. "I can't control them."

You're feeling sorry for Ellie, aren't you?

I'm not! Dad and I were doing just fine, then Ellie comes and ruins everything, with pink Christmas trees and stupid laundry bags. Not to mention the stinky little Blob…

Plus she has these mad rules! Like in the Easter holidays she says I can only watch *one* DVD a day, then I've got to amuse myself!

"But it's *boring* now Dad's back at work!" I moan.

"Then play outside," she says firmly.

I storm into the garden. A tiny frog unexpectedly pings out of the fish pond, giving us both a fright.

We get frogs in our garden every spring. I feel a nasty smile spreading across my face.

Ellie's REALLY scared of frogs!

Later I tiptoe into the house carrying an old bucket. Can you guess what's inside? Yess! Teeny-tiny, squirmy, slimy baby frogs!

I quickly empty them into the coats cupboard and close the door.

"Ellie!" I shout upstairs.

My stepmum comes downstairs with the Blob.

"Remember those special tulips you planted in the garden?" I say brightly. "They're coming up. Want to see?"

My stepmum falls for it.

"OK," she beams. "You take Joe while I get his jacket."

I grasp the Blob cautiously around its blobby middle.

"Don't worry, he won't explode!" Ellie laughs.

She opens the cupboard door, sees the frogs and shrieks.

I howl with laughter as baby frogs go hopping everywhere like tiny clockwork toys!

Ellie lets out another shriek as one hops on to her slipper.

"You've gone TOO far, Honey Hope!" she yells. "Go to your room, NOW!"

"I was just GOING!" I yell back. "Can't you take a JOKE!"

I thunder up the stairs.

For a moment I hear little hippity-hoppity sounds behind me.

But I must have frogs on the brain because when I swing round, there's nothing there.

7.
Frog Sandwiches

This is where my weird story gets even weirder!

You know the frog on the stairs that wasn't there?

The minute I come out of my room, it's back

– *hoppity squelch*, *hoppity squelch* – like clammy little feet hopping along behind me.

Only each time I turn round there's nothing there!

The invisible frog follows me everywhere – to the swimming pool, to the park. Everywhere I go, it follows.

Ellie doesn't seem to notice anything wrong.

"Can't you hear it?" I ask Ellie.

"Hear what, sweetie?"

"That noise like a frog hopping."

ZZZzzzz

Ellie gives me a strange look.

I gulp.

"You don't think I'm being, you know, *haunted*?

"Can you have frog ghosts?" She laughs. "Honey, sorry, even I'm not falling for that one!"

I start to think I'm going crazy.

There's only one place where I can get any peace. The frog noises never once follow me into my room. I start spending a LOT of time alone with my fishes.

The night before school starts I lie awake, whispering, "Please please *please* don't let it follow me to school."

Next morning I stumble to the bathroom. Halfway across the landing, I hear the squelches I've come to dread. It's like I'm trapped in a bad dream and there's no way out.

Don't try to imagine how it feels to be trailed round your school by a frog that isn't there. You can't.

Somehow I struggle through the morning. At dinner time I have to share a table with Bella, Sam and Charlie. They glance up warily, then go back to their conversation.

I open my lunchbox – and scream.

There's a tiny frog sitting on my sandwich!!

I can't speak. I just point and go on screaming.

"What's the matter?" Bella asks.

"Slug in her lettuce?" Sam suggests.

"What a shame," clowns Charlie.

No one can see the frog except me.

I take a close look at my sandwich.

The frog chuckles. "Got you going, didn't I?"

It's Lilac Peabody!

I'm ready to explode.

"Ooh you – you *big* PIG! You've been playing magic tricks on me!"

"I didn't think you believed in magic," the frog teases.

"Who's she calling a pig?" Sam asks everyone.

I'm almost stamping. "I HATE you Lola Beanpole! First you ruined my holiday and now you've ruined my sandwich!"

"My name's Lilac Peabody," the little frog reminds me calmly, "and how did I ruin your sandwich? I didn't even have a nibble!"

"I don't care what your stupid name is!" I scream. "You *sat* on my sandwich with your squelchy little bum!"

"Ah, don't get mad! Let's kiss and make up!" Lilac puckers her froggy lips.

"I wouldn't kiss you for a million pounds!" I scream.

"We're not too crazy about kissing her either," Charlie sniggers to Sam.

But Bella tells the boys to leave me alone, then she whispers something I can't hear.

That night I toss and turn, but I can't find a cool place on my pillows. My throat hurts and I've got these horrible feelings churning inside me. It's like my boiling-lava feelings, except I don't seem to have enough energy to explode.

Suddenly, with a soft WHOOSH, Lilac Peabody appears.

"I want you to know that I never ONCE came into your room until now," she says earnestly. "I *totally* respected your wishes."

"So why are you here?"

My throat is so sore my voice sounds like a croak.

Lilac Peabody smiles. "In my world, friends always look after each other when they're sick."

"Why are you being nice?" I ask feebly.

"I'm always nice," she says in surprise.

"No, you're not," I croak. "That frog trick was super mean."

"I had to get your attention somehow!" she sighs. "You're my toughest case yet, Honeysuckle Hope!"

"So why bother?" I say bleakly. "You can't help me. You can't bring my mum back. No magic can make that happen."

Suddenly I start to cry. My body shakes with huge sobs that actually hurt my chest. I cry like I've never cried before. I didn't even know I had that many tears in me.

Lilac strokes my hot face with a cool, rather fizzy, hand.

Ellie hears me crying and hurries in. She feels my forehead and calls to Dad, who immediately phones our doctor.

Doctor Moody makes me stick out my tongue and scribbles a prescription.

When the grown-ups have gone, Lilac scribbles her own prescription and shows it to me. ***One tablespoon of magic to be taken three times a day after meals.***

"You don't give up, do you?" I say weakly.

"Why would I do that?" she asks in surprise. "You're an incredibly special girl, Honey Hope."

"Mum and Dad gave me the wrong name," I sniffle. "Maybe I was sweet when I was little, but I'm not sweet any more. I'm not even hopeful."

"You're still sweet on the inside," she tells me. "After your mum died, it probably felt too scary to let the sweetness out. But you won't always feel so scared and lonely."

"How do you know?" I whisper.

She taps her nose. "Special Powers! Now try to sleep."

"Don't go," I hear myself say.

"I'm not going anywhere," she promises. She

starts singing softly under her breath. Not to be rude, but Lilac can't sing for peanuts. Yet her weird lullaby makes me feel more peaceful than I've felt for months…

In the middle of the night, I wake feeling thirsty. My room is still filled with a silvery glow. I prop myself up on my elbows. Lilac Peabody is sitting beside my aquarium. My fish are gazing at her adoringly.

They totally trust her, I think, amazed.

In a funny way that helps me to trust her too.

8.
Sweet Side Out

Next day I still feel weak and wobbly, so Ellie keeps me at home for a few more days until she's sure I'm over my bug.

On the last day I ask if I can bake some cakes

to take to school.

"What a lovely idea!" she beams.

While the cakes are in
the oven, Ellie shows
me how to make
her special icing.
The kitchen fills
with baking smells.

At last my cakes
are ready. When they're
cool, I spoon on icing, then decorate them with
tiny sugar flowers.

I'm suddenly nervous. I want to show my
sweet side, like Lilac says, but it feels really scary.

Next day at break, I shyly offer one of my
cakes to Lara.

"Did you make these yourself?" asks her new
friend, Michelle.

I nod proudly.

Michelle briskly knocks the cake out of Lara's hand. "My friend doesn't want one of your poisonous cakes thanks!"

When I get home, I give Ellie the empty tin.

"You were popular," she laughs.

"Yeah, I was," I fib.

I'm too ashamed to say I put the cakes in the bin. Ellie has loads of friends. She doesn't know what it's like to be all alone.

Lilac Peabody comes after everyone else is asleep.

"The cake plan didn't work, huh?" she sighs.

"I wanted to let my sweet side out," I say

 miserably, "but no one would let me!"

"Not even Sam and Charlie?" she says in surprise. "Those boys are complete dustbins!"

I feel myself going red. "I didn't ask them. When they saw me offering cakes to everyone, they started whispering to Bella."

"Maybe they were whispering something nice?" Lilac suggests.

"Yeah right! Like anyone would be nice about the school bully!"

My voice does a sudden wobble. "Now I'll have to be a bully for the rest of my life!"

"You could be right," Lilac agrees.

I stare at her as if I've been slapped. "You're not supposed to say that! You said you were my friend!"

"It's your life," she chuckles. "You're in charge – not me."

Hot tears fill my eyes. "Yes, that's right Lilac. It's my life, and it's really mean to laugh at me!"

Lilac looks interested. "Do you want me to cry? Because you've turned your life into a sad story about a poor lonely girl called Honeysuckle Hope who nobody loves?"

I burst into tears. "But I *am* lonely, and nobody *does* love me!"

"Honey, that's just not true! There are *three* people here in this house who love you very much!"

"Like who?" I snivel.

"Your dad for one. His whole life fell apart when your mum died, but he put it back together because of *you*, Honey!"

New tears spill down my face. "My dad's got a new family now."

"It's *your* family too," Lilac reminds me. "Haven't you noticed how Joe breaks into huge smiles every time he sees you?"

"Joe also smiles at dogs and fire engines," I point out tearily. "And Ellie only puts up with me because of Dad."

"Come with me," Lilac says firmly. "It's time for a history lesson."

I tiptoe after her as she flits downstairs and into the sitting room. The dark room makes Lilac's starry glow seem extra bright.

I watch in bewilderment as she zooms back and forth along the shelf where Dad and Ellie keep the photo albums. What *is* Lilac Peabody up to?

"This is the one!" Lilac is hovering in front of a battered leather album that I don't remember seeing before.

I lift the album down and open it.

The first snap shows a scared little girl in a huge school uniform, standing in front of an ugly building. A sign says *Whitegrove Boarding School for Girls*. The little girl is clutching a large teddy bear.

"The Blob's got a bear just like that one," I whisper.

"It's the same bear," Lilac says softly. "That little girl is your stepmum."

"That's *Ellie*! Her parents sent her to boarding school! Were they *crazy*! She's like four years old!"

Lilac shakes her head. "I'd never known such a

lonely little girl." She gives me a meaningful look. "Until I met you."

My mouth falls open. "You helped Ellie?"

Lilac just looks at me with her huge luminous eyes that are far too wise to be human. "That's inside info," she says.

We go back to looking at the frightened little four-year-old who grew up to be my stepmum.

"But why didn't she *tell* me," I burst out.

Lilac pats my cheek and my whole face goes fizzy like fizzy lemonade. "Maybe you didn't give her a chance?" she suggests.

It's true.

I never gave Ellie a chance – not once.

✳

I don't tell Ellie I know about her and Lilac Peabody. Lilac says she probably doesn't even remember. I say I found the picture when I was hunting out info for a school project.

"I didn't damage it, I swear!" I say earnestly.

I put it carefully on the kitchen table.

My stepmum hides her face, laughing. "You should have torn it up! Ugh! That hideous uniform!"

I take a breath. "You look so sad in the picture."

Ellie sighs. "I was sad. I'm afraid my parents didn't want me around that much." She gives me a warm smile. "Still — I lucked out in the end!"

I look away, "You didn't luck out with me."

"Sweetie, don't! Losing your mum must have been terrible. No one expects you to get over that overnight."

My chin wobbles. "I want to change back to the nice Honey, I do, but I can't remember how!"

Ellie makes me look at her. "Honeysuckle

Hope," she says firmly, "don't you know your dad and I love you just the way you are?"

"That's not what you said before," I choke.

My stepmum pulls me on to her lap and hugs me. "I admit I lost it over those frogs!" she chuckles. "But I'd rather have you *with* frogs than not have you at all!"

I'm crying so hard that Ellie's jumper is getting wet.

"Tell me what to do, Ellie," I sob. "I don't know what to do."

9.
The Magic's Just Beginning

"I can't believe I agreed to go!" I moan to Lilac a few days later. I'm crashing about, opening and shutting drawers, getting myself into a real grump. "Kids from my school are going to be there. It'll be a nightmare."

"You're right," Lilac says calmly. "I think you should forget all about it and stay quietly at home with your fish."

"Don't make fun of me, Louisa Peabrain!" I pull a hideous face.

Lilac pulls an even more hideous face. "It's your life, Honey!"

"Yeah, yeah, I'm in charge now – blah blah!"

"Smart girl – you're catching on," she chuckles.

"If I'm so smart why am I going to a picnic for Teddy Bears!" I complain, struggling into my jeans.

"I don't know. Why are you?"

Lilac gives me a sudden searching look. It's like she's seeing all of me at once, the sad girl who lost her mum, the bad girl who didn't believe in magic and the new sweet Honeysuckle that I wanted to be all along.

My voice goes husky. "Maybe I really want to change?"

"Maybe you do," she says softly.

Downstairs, Dad is spooning some kind of gloop into the Blob. "Hi, Honey Bun!" He smiles. "I hear you're going to the Mothers and Toddlers Picnic with Ellie and Joe?" He tries not to sound surprised.

I jab my finger at the flier on the fridge.

"Duh! It says 'Family Event', Dad! I *am* in this family, you know." I give him a mischievous grin. "Plus Ellie promised she'd take me clothes shopping afterwards!"

"Oh, real girl stuff." He laughs.

Later I push Joe's buggy through the park with a crowd of mums and little pre-schoolers. All the toddlers have brought their favourite teddies to the picnic. Joe is proudly clutching Ellie's battered old ted.

The birds are singing, the sun is shining and we're moving as slowly as a family of snails. Joe keeps dropping his teddy, plus Ellie constantly stops to gossip to other mums.

"At this rate the teddies will starve to death," I tell Joe grumpily.

Ellie stops to natter again. "Do you mind taking him to the swings?" she calls.

"OK!" I sigh.

I start towards the toddler's play area. My heart sinks as I see my ex-best friend Lara coming down the path.

To my amazement she stops to talk. "Is that your brother?" she asks shyly. "He's sweet!"

I look down at the small curly-haired figure in the buggy.

She's right, I realise in surprise.

Joe isn't a bald blob any more. He's a cute little boy. Joe sees me looking and gives me a beaming smile. Suddenly I'm smiling back.

"Hello Joe Hope," I say softly.

It's the first time I've called my brother by his name.

Lara seems to be working up the courage to say something. "About those cakes," she blurts. "Michelle shouldn't have—"

"Don't worry about it," I say quickly.

"She thought you were just playing a trick." Lara looks upset. "Honey, I'm so sorry."

"It's OK.

I totally understand why she did it."

Lara shakes her head. Her eyes are suddenly full of tears. "No, I mean how I treated you after… I didn't know what to—"

I swallow. "Yeah, well, probably I didn't either."

We give each other shy smiles.

"So I'll see you around?" she says awkwardly.

"Yeah definitely," I tell her.

As I push open the gate to the toddlers' playground, the first person I see is Bella pushing her little sister in a baby swing.

The boys are with her. Charlie is helping his little sister climb the steps to the slide.

I ignore them and march over to one of the swings. To my surprise Sam comes and steadies it for me. "What's your brother's name?" he asks politely. "Joe," I mumble.

Bella and the boys exchange glances.

"My parents couldn't agree on my little sister's name," Bella says in a casual voice. "She ended up being called Lily-Louisa Lilac Lucy Bright." Bella shoots me a look. "I just wanted to call her Lilac."

Magic tingles are going down my spine, but I'm scared I'll look stupid. Suppose Bella's talking about a different Lilac?

Sam clears his throat. "Lilac's sort of a friend of ours," he says in a hinting voice.

"We were wondering if you knew her too," Charlie chips in.

"Lilac helped us loads," Bella says earnestly,

"but we had to go through some nutty stuff first!"

"I bet you never had a frog in your lunchbox!" I blurt out without thinking.

Bella gasps. "You poor thing! No wonder you screamed!"

I start to laugh. "It's my own fault! I made my room into a magic-free zone. She had to get through to me somehow!"

Suddenly we're all swapping Lilac Peabody stories.

"I wished to be cured of my stage fright," giggles Bella. "Lilac made me dance around with my knickers on my head. And it *worked*!"

"I wished to have a birthday party just once," sighs Sam.

"I just wanted to survive my weird family." Charlie grins.

"I didn't believe in wishes full stop," I tell them. "I tried wishing when my mum was ill and it didn't work."

Bella's eyes go huge. "Honey, I don't think you can wish about—"

"I know that now," I interrupt quickly. "I was a bit mixed up."

The park is filling up with families. The mums get busy unpacking picnic baskets. Toddlers feed tiny sandwiches to their teddies, while their big brothers and sisters do handstands on the grass.

I have a daring brainwave. "My stepmum

always brings way too much food," I say shyly. "I don't suppose you guys would share it?"

I get a fizzy sensation in the ends of my hair, as if a magic somebody has just zoomed over my head.

A familiar voice chuckles, "Congratulations, Honey! You just got your sweetness back!"

I'm the only one who hears Lilac's voice but Bella and the boys look up with amazed expressions as if their hair feels fizzy too. Even Joe and Lily-Louisa look up.

"That was *her*," whispers Sam.

And suddenly we're all gazing up at the clear blue sky, longing for a last glimpse of that mysterious little busybody.

We're four completely different kids, but it's like we all belong to the same crazy family. Lilac Peabody touched us with her magic Powers. Now we'll never be the same.

A shimmery card floats down from the sky.

I pick it up and my skin breaks into goose bumps.

It's the same card I tore up at the wedding; you can see the join.

I can hear Bella and the others discussing Lilac Peabody.

"You don't think she was trying to get us together the whole time?" Bella says slowly.

Sam gives an amazed chuckle. "Wouldn't that be just like her!"

"You mean the magic isn't *over*!" Charlie breathes.

Ellie is walking towards us with the picnic basket. She waves and I wave back.

I turn to my friends. "No, it isn't over!"

I show them the new message on the back of Lilac's card.

"*The magic is just beginning*," Bella reads in an astonished voice.

And I can't stop smiling, because I know it's true.

I never felt so sure of anything in my life.